The Good Companion

The Good Companion

written by JOAN SKOGAN

illustrated by STEPHEN McCALLUM

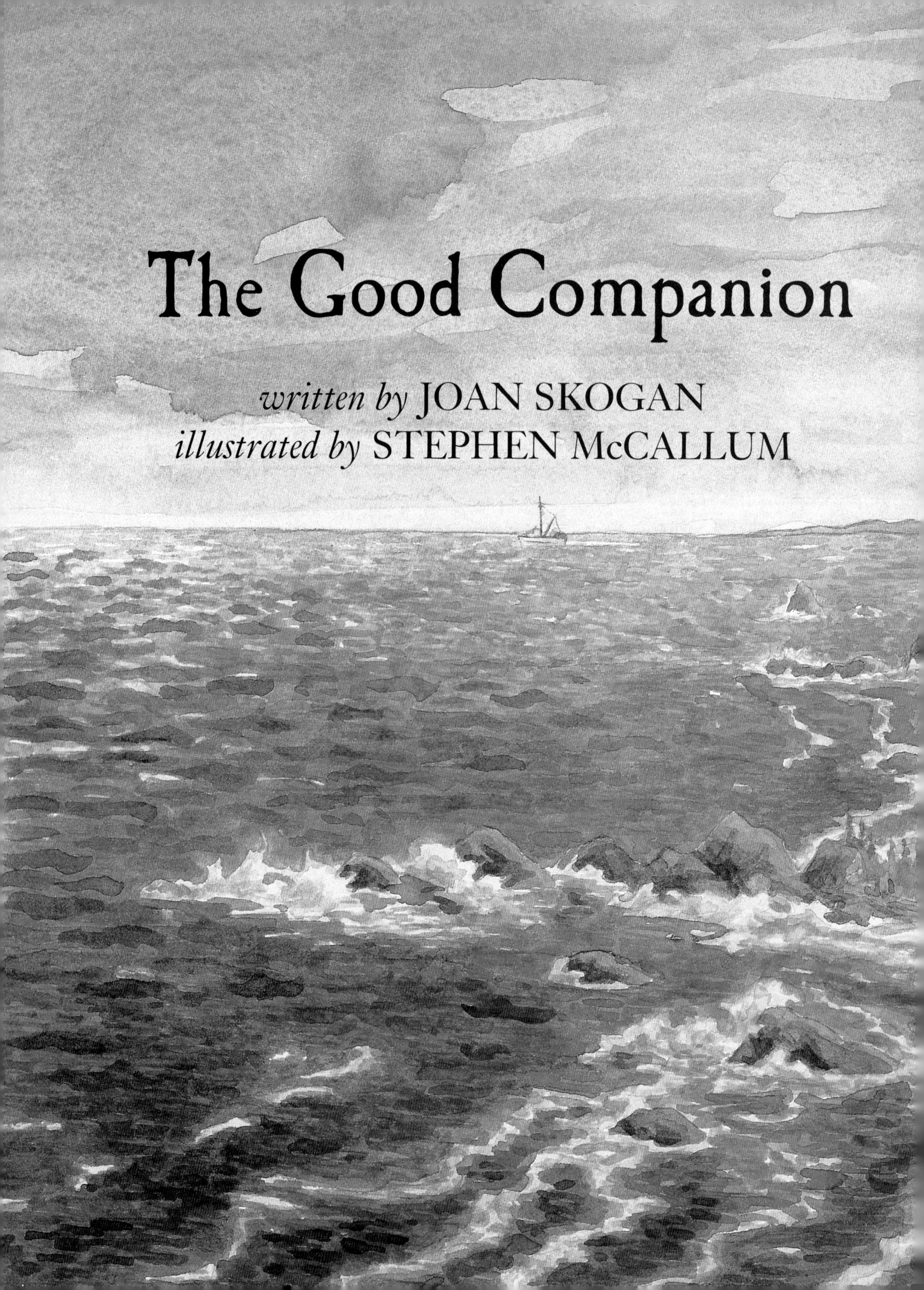

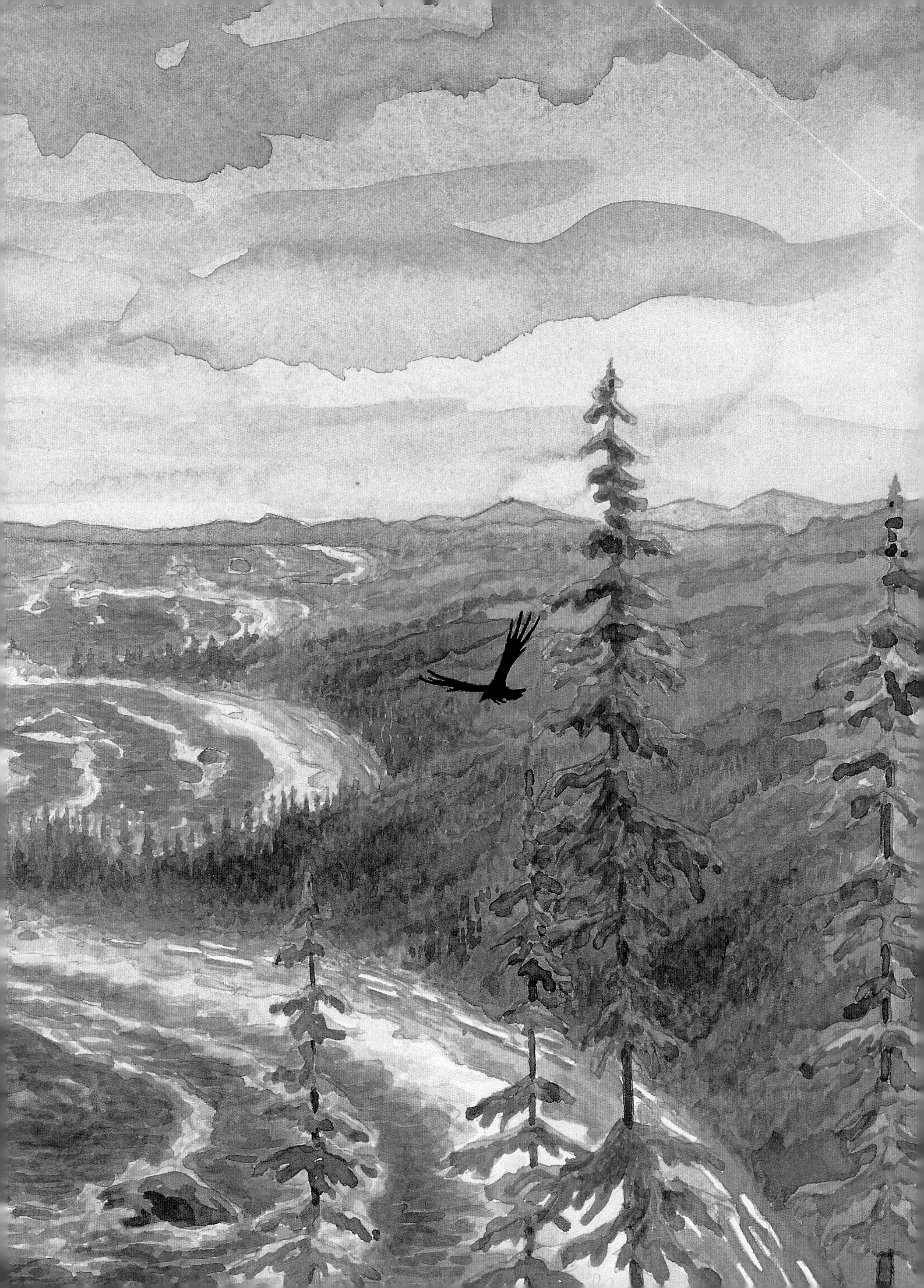

EARLY one winter-gray morning the *Good Companion* left harbor, bound for the deepwater fishing grounds offshore.

The captain scarcely noticed the wind pushing against his boat or the rain blurring the wheelhouse windows. He and his crew worked one fishing trip after another in hard weather. They fished long days, then slept easily on rolling seas far from home.

The galley was always warm. The fish holds were usually full when they returned to port. The captain, the cook, the engineer and the two deckhands trusted the *Good Companion* and her luck.

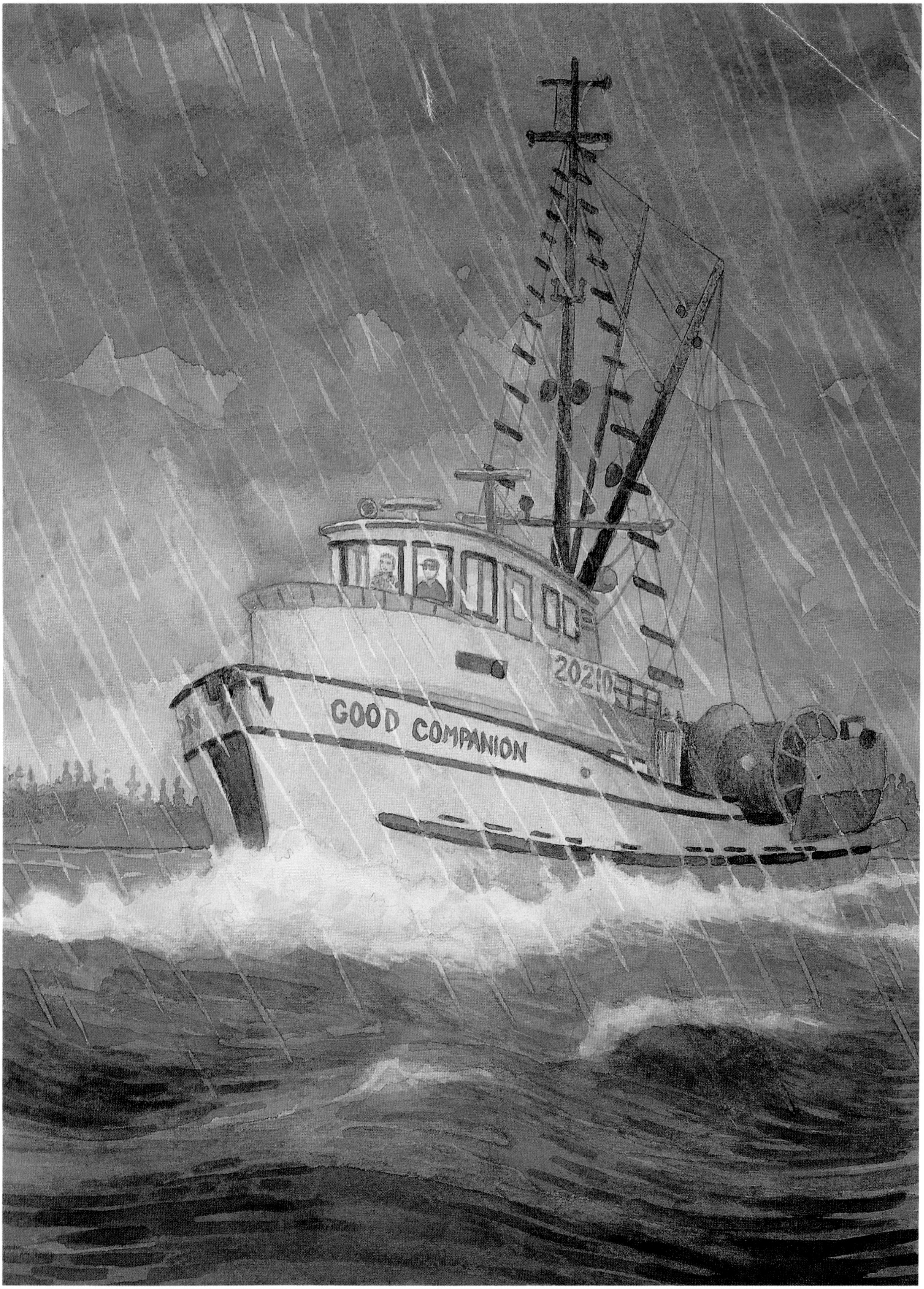
20210
GOOD COMPANION

The captain took no chances with the *Good Companion*'s sea luck. He made sure that the crew's coffee cups, which hung in a row above the sink, faced inboard so as not to pour luck over the side. He allowed no cans to be opened upside down for fear of overturning the boat. No whistling that could call up a wind. No black suitcases to bring a doctor or death on board. No fishing trips began on Friday, the unluckiest day of the week. No sly, water-shy cats. No women: women belonged to home and the land.

And no changes. Change might disturb his boat's luck, the captain thought. New chart courses, new fishing grounds, new crew members and newfangled food were strangers to the *Good Companion*. The wind changed from one quarter to another. Tides rose, slacked and fell, then rose again. The ocean crashed or calmed, and fish schools moved from one feeding place to the next. These changes were enough for the captain.

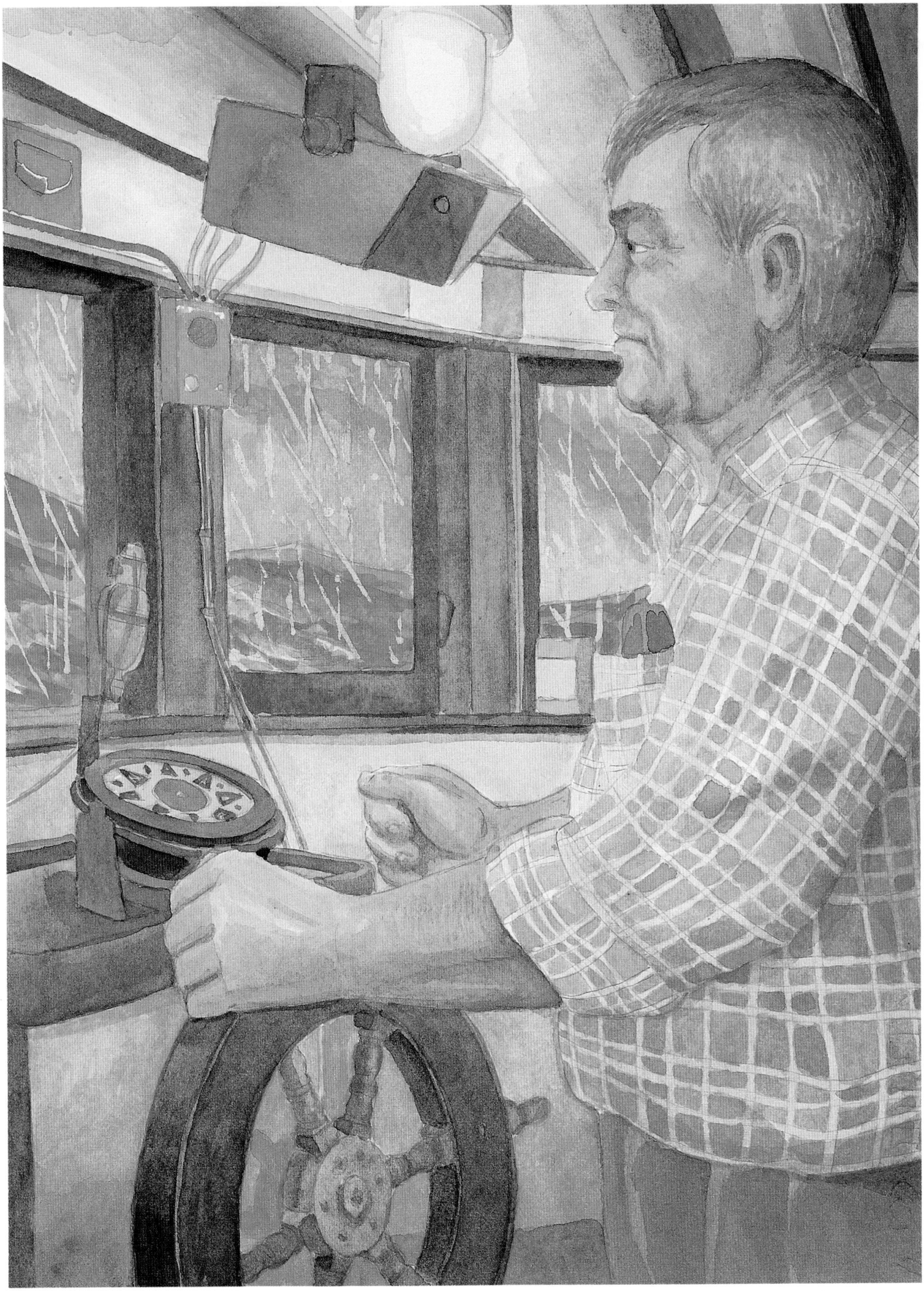

When daylight faded on the first afternoon of the trip, the *Good Companion* was running alone in a northwest gale. One last empty rock island was all the land that lay in sight before the open sea. The captain steered for shelter in the island's bay.

"No sense taking a beating all night," he called back to the cook standing by the stove, minding his sliding pots.

The boat swayed up to the head of the bay, and the wind became a distant scream behind her. The outside swells broke down to low, choppy waves. On the bow the deckhands shivered as they dropped the anchor into dark water. The yellow glow from the *Good Companion*'s galley windows was the only sign of light or life in the bay.

"Dinner's ready," the cook called, and the fishermen sat down in the places where they always sat around the ridge-edged table. The galley was as warm as ever. Dinner was the same meal the cook made on the first night of every trip: ham with pineapple rings, scalloped potatoes, niblets corn, coleslaw and white rolls. Raisin pie from the bakery in town for dessert.

"Scalloped potatoes are my favorite," the youngest deckhand said, as he always did. As he reached for the last helping, a voice cried out from the blackness beyond the boat.

The men stared at each other. "Must have been the wind," the cook whispered. "Nobody's out here except us."

"Hallo up there!"

Knives and forks fell to the table. "Impossible," the captain announced. He marched out to the deck with his crew behind him.

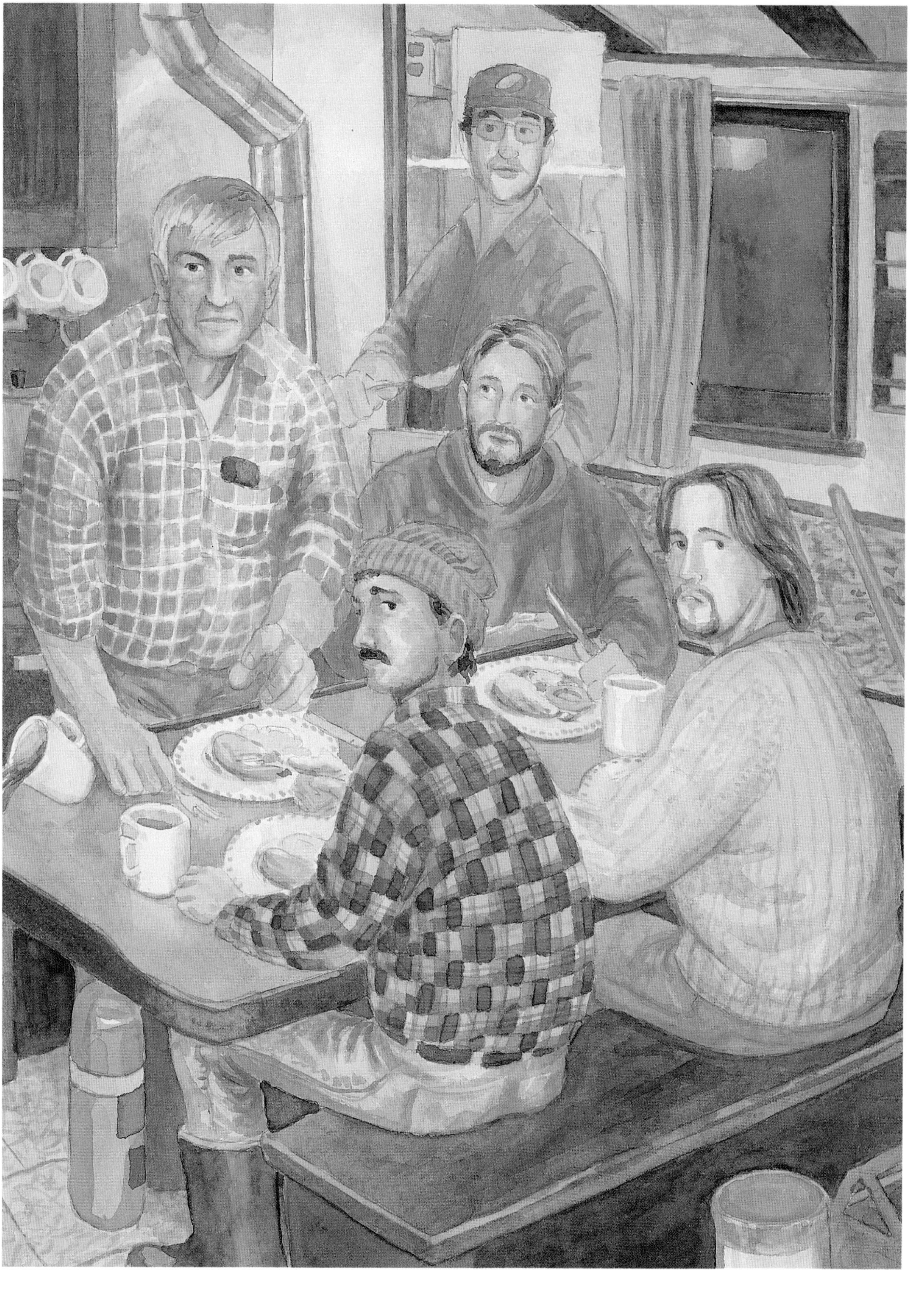

On the dark sea below, a girl whose long red hair floated around her shoulders like feathery seaweed sat in a wooden skiff with water over the floorboards. The captain looked long and hard at the girl in her half-swamped skiff alongside his boat in the only bay on the last island before open water.

"Can I come up?" she called.

No, the captain wanted to say. No women or strangers wanted on board. Go away, whoever you are. Whatever you are. But the deckhands had already let down the rope ladder, and a line for the skiff. All too soon the girl stood on the deck of the *Good Companion* in her sea-splashed clothes and soaked shoes.

The engineer opened the galley door for her. She sat down on the end of the outside bench, where no one else ever sat. The cook cut some ham and heaped it on the plate. "And scalloped potatoes," she said, "my favorite." The youngest deckhand passed her the last helping.

The girl ate all the food left on the table, and two pieces of raisin pie, while the cook, the engineer and the deckhands watched. The captain did not look at her. When she had finished eating, the captain glared at the light over the galley table and demanded, "What's a woman doing by herself on a piece of rock with nothing but the ocean around it?"

The girl's head drooped, and the tangled hair covered her face. "Tired out," the cook decided. "She'd better stay on here tonight."

The captain sighed and mumbled under his breath about women and luck, while the engineer went down to clear his fuel pump parts off the spare bunk. The deckhands found an extra sleeping bag, which smelled like fish and diesel oil. The cook led the girl to the ladder.

In the fo'c's'le, beneath the waterline, the girl crawled into the sleeping bag on the spare bunk. She and the cook listened to the anchor chain rattling along the hull and to the skiff knocking softly on the side of the *Good Companion*. The girl placed her hand flat on the bulkhead by her pillow, as if to feel the green weight of the sea moving against it, and smiled.

"Where did you come from?" the cook asked. But the girl's eyes were closed and she did not answer. The cook spread a blanket over the sleeping bag and left her alone.

Up in the galley, the captain waited to hear what the cook had discovered about the redheaded girl. The cook stood by the window above the sink, looking out into the night. He touched the cold glass and listened to the wind howl past the mouth of the bay. Then he crossed his fingers and told the captain a lie. "She flew up to the island last summer with some sportsfish people from the city," he said as he tied the girl's drenched, salt-smelling shoes to the drying line over the stove. "Wouldn't go back with them."

"Fool," the captain growled. He washed his coffee cup and hung it in line with the others. The cook turned down the stove and they went to bed.

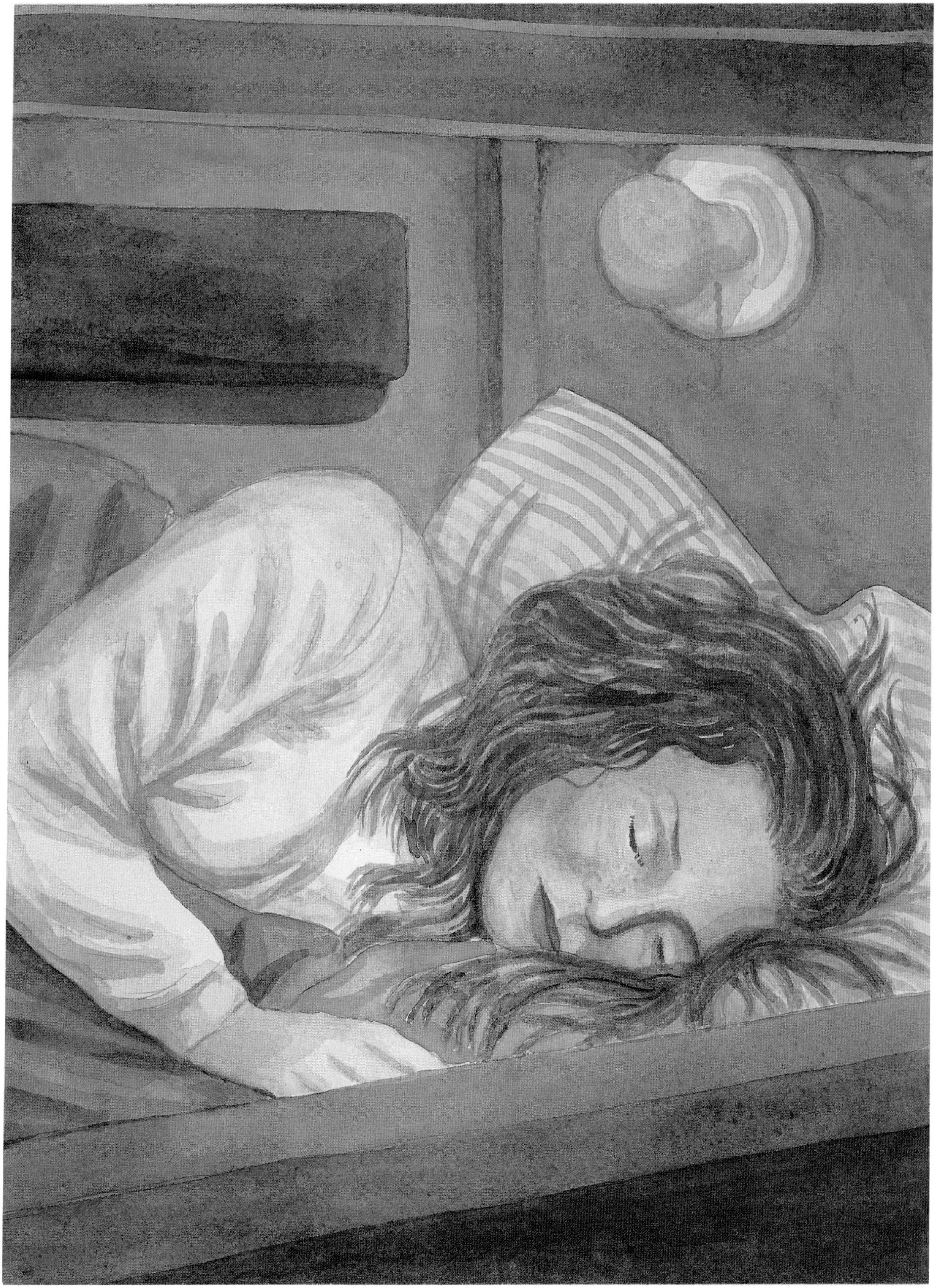

In the night the *Good Companion* moved restlessly on her anchor chain, pulled by the tide rushing from the bay to the wild ocean outside. The tide slacked before dawn, and the girl awoke in her fo'c's'le bunk. She put her hand on the bulkhead beside her, as if to be sure that the waters of the bay were truly almost still.

She slept again. In the stillness below the waterline, she dreamed the same dream as the captain, the cook, the engineer and the two deckhands in their cabins up top. The shared dream carried the fishermen and the redheaded girl together on a boat which became a bird that flew high above a storm, then floated easily on the great swells of the sea.

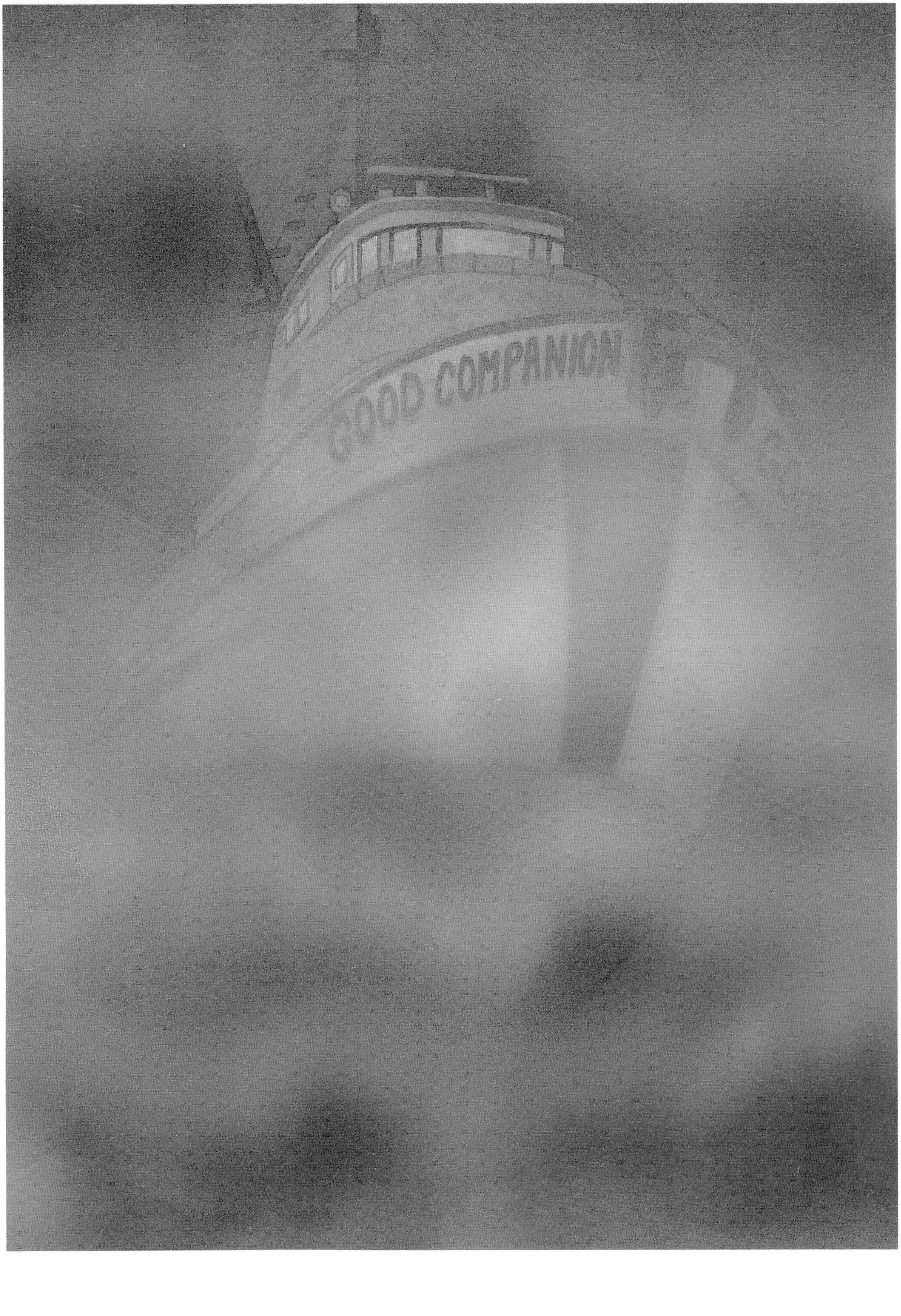
GOOD COMPANION

In the morning, no one talked about the dream. The cook fried eggs, bacon and pancakes while the girl buttered a stack of toast. Breakfast disappeared quickly, except for the captain's toast, which he did not touch. Then the girl helped the deckhands with the dishes.

The captain stepped out on deck to look at the sinking skiff tied to his stern. He zipped his jacket against the chill, damp air, then lifted his binoculars to scan the rocky shores of the bay. He saw the tilted shack where the girl had been living. He saw the door the wind had blown open.

In the wheelhouse he tuned the radio to the marine weather report. *Northwest winds continuing on outside waters … dropping to thirty-five knots by midday … two to three meter swells … freezing rain.* The captain leaned into the galley. "Cut that skiff loose. Fire up the engine." Then, gloomily, "She'll have to come with us, luck or no luck. We'll snag both nets and haul nothing but water now."

But no nets snagged or came up empty. The gale blew further out to sea while the fishermen towed their gear on the deepwater fishing grounds and hauled the nets back full of fish day after day. The captain watched his charts and ignored the redheaded girl.

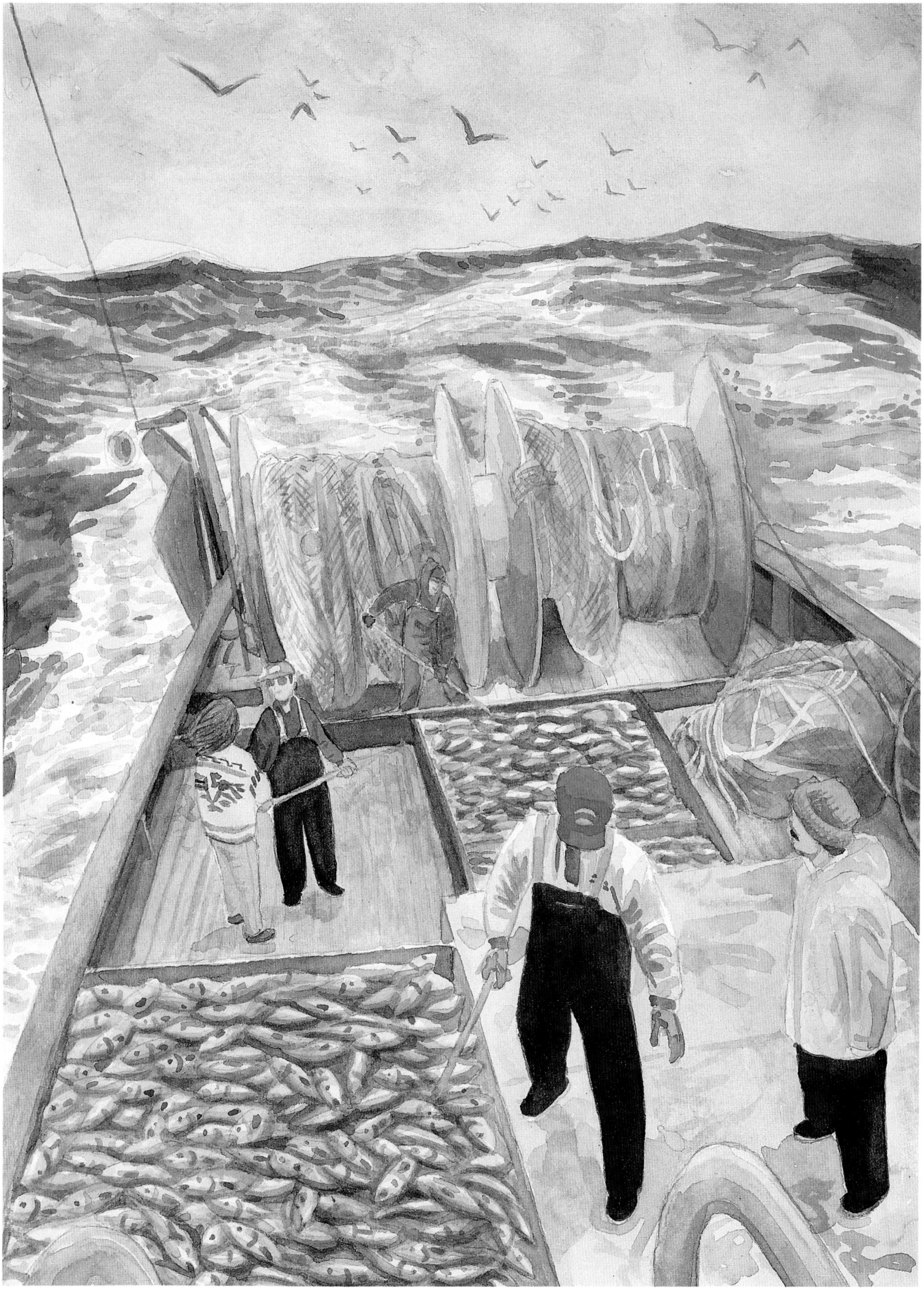

The girl learned to clean fish on deck and laughed at the deckhands' jokes. She sang "Red River Valley" with the engineer because it was the only song he knew. The captain never spoke a word to her. She baked a chocolate cake, but he wouldn't eat it. "All the more for us," said the engineer, who took four pieces.

For nine days the boat worked on the open seas and no one on board slept long enough to dream. On the tenth day, the fish holds were full and the *Good Companion* began her long run back to port. The engineer took the first wheel turn, singing "Red River Valley" in time with the engines. In the galley the girl sat with the cook on the outside bench, peeling potatoes, while the captain at the far end of the table scratched fish prices on a paper napkin. Beside him the deckhands ate popcorn and played Yahtzee with dice so old their corners were round.

After supper, when everyone was asleep except for the cook on the wheel and the captain standing beside him, the cook said, "You could let her stay on board for a while. Until she rests up. You can't say she's been bad luck."

"Yet," said the captain. "Hasn't been bad luck yet. She's a woman. No women on boats." And he went to his cabin.

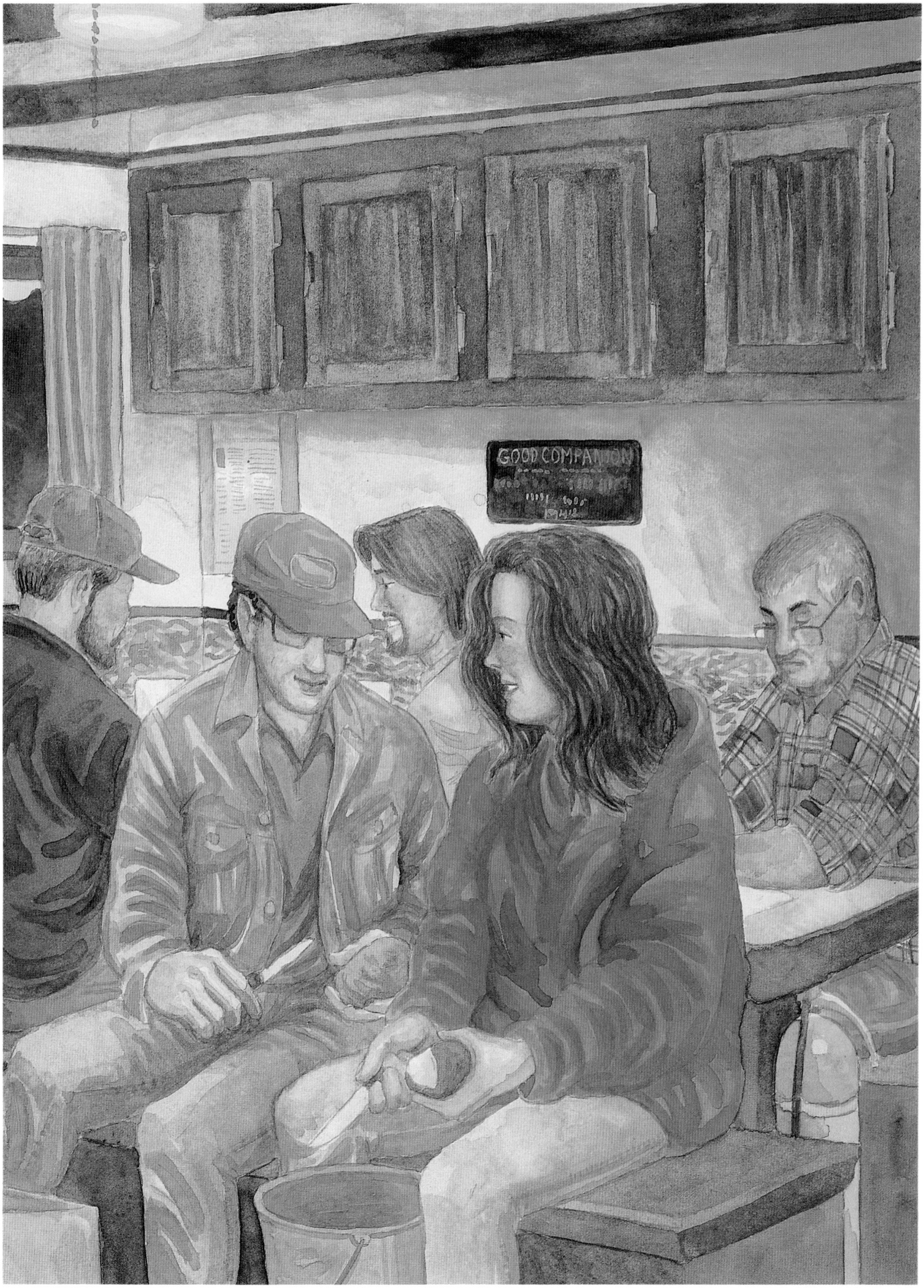
GOOD COMPANION

The harbor lights appeared before the sky showed any sign of day. The captain got up to steer the *Good Companion* past the ferry wharf and the floats to the fish dock. The deckhands tied the mooring lines to the pilings, the engineer shut down the engines and the boat was silent for the first time since she had stood at anchor in the faraway bay.

The crew gathered on deck around the redheaded girl, and she looked carefully at each of them. "Thank you," she said and reached for their hands. Both deckhands shook hands with her at the same time. The engineer gave her a greasy hug.

The cook asked, "Where will you go now?" She didn't answer, only held out her hand to the captain standing by the galley door, but he stepped back from her and would not take her hand.

She climbed up on the deck rail and took hold of the ladder dangling from the dock above. For an instant she stood with one foot still on the *Good Companion* and one foot on the first steel rung of the ladder.

The captain, his feet firm on his own deck, thought he saw the girl and the dock and the land itself leaving the *Good Companion*, spinning faster and faster away from his boat. "Impossible," he muttered to himself. He turned to walk up to the wheelhouse. "Be ready to unload at six," he shouted over his shoulder.

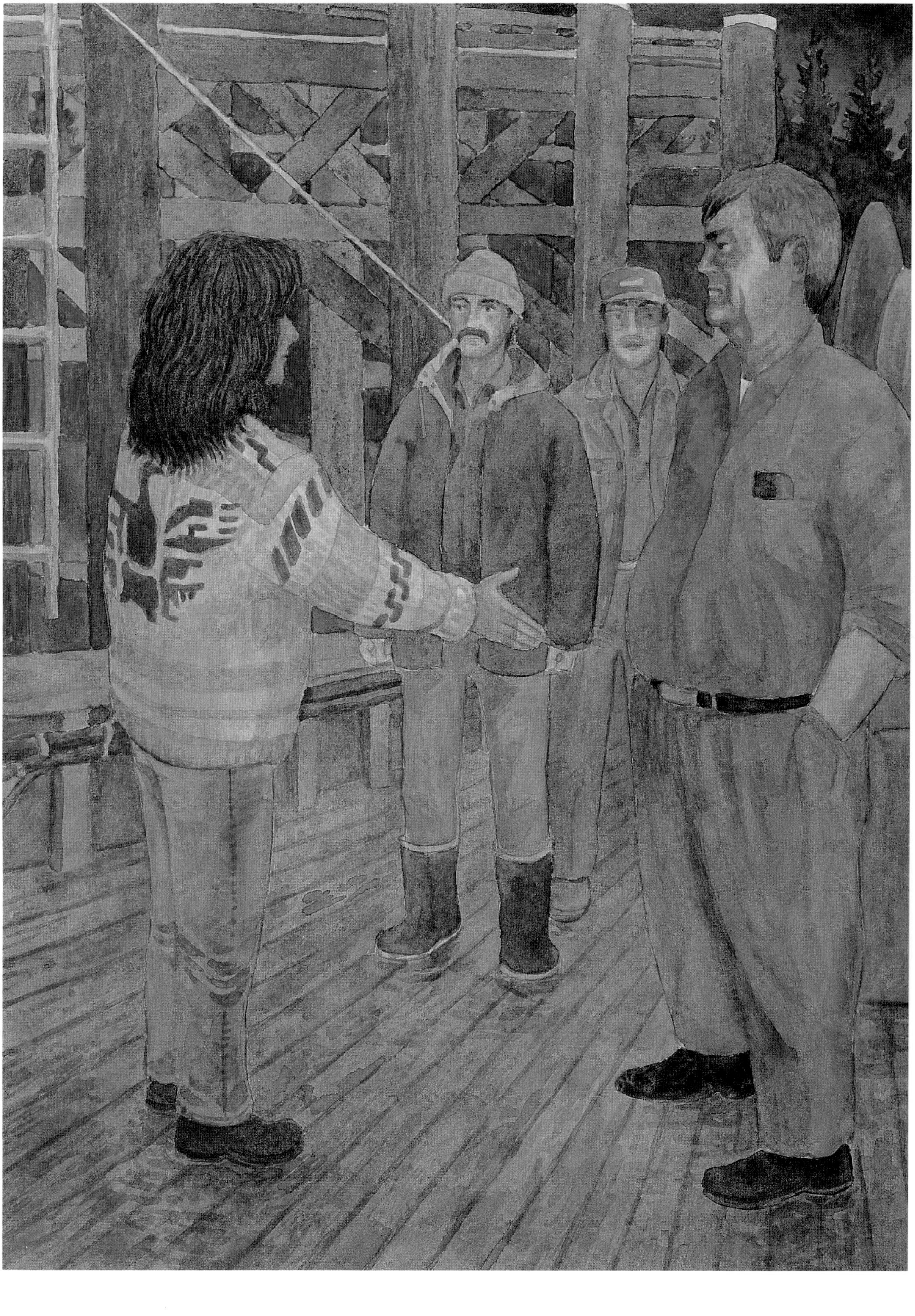

No one on the *Good Companion* saw or heard of the redheaded girl as winter turned to spring, then summer, fall and winter again. The wind, the sea and the schools of fish changed in ways the captain and his men already knew.

The men ate ham with pineapple rings, scalloped potatoes, niblets corn, coleslaw and white rolls, with raisin pie for dessert the first night of every trip. Sometimes the fish holds were full. Sometimes not. Fish prices rose, dropped, then steadied.

The captain spoke only to give orders. The engineer did not sing "Red River Valley" much any more. Only the redheaded girl had known all the words. The deckhands were quieter and told no jokes. There was no one to laugh at them. The cook sighed now and then, wondering what had happened to the girl who had come out of the darkness in a leaky skiff the night the wind whistled past the mouth of the bay.

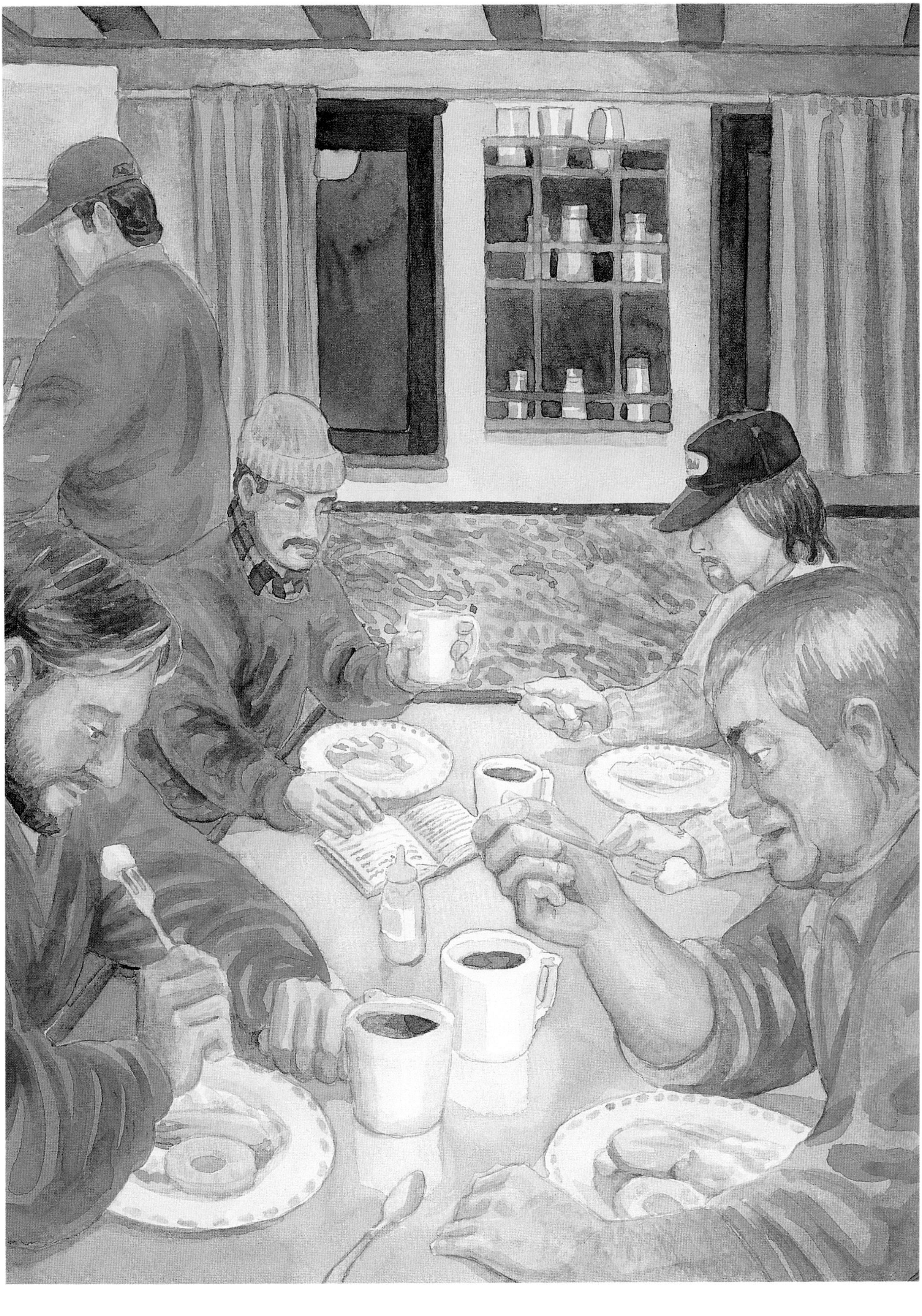

One winter morning the *Good Companion* set out again for the deepwater fishing grounds. Rain slashed the wheelhouse windows as the boat pushed against a rising gale late into the afternoon. The pots on the stove slid into the siderails. The ham in the oven slanted in its pan, and the cook's potatoes leaped from the sink before he could wash them.

When the last empty rock island was the only land to be seen in the flying spray, the captain remembered the redheaded girl. He remembered that she had cleaned his fish on deck and got along with the crew and not talked too much. He remembered that the *Good Companion* had not lost luck when she was onboard. And he remembered she was a woman.

"Tie the gear down," he shouted to the crew. And he steered around the island to make for the open sea.

The boat slowed at first on the wider, wilder water, then staggered and began to roll hard. The cook rescued his potatoes and set dinner plates over dampened dish cloths on the galley table to keep them from sliding. The *Good Companion* pounded on, slamming from side to side. The coffee cups trembled on their hooks and the huge enamel coffee pot crashed to the floor.

The captain struggled with all his strength to turn the boat to face the wind and sea head-on so she could regain some stability. But again and again she was pushed broadside to the white-capped swells. Water poured green over the wheelhouse windows, then rushed the length of the deck.

Down below the engineer cursed his automatic pumps, his hand pumps and all pumps ever made. The deckhands' lips quivered as they crammed themselves into a corner of the wheelhouse beside the captain. The cook sat on the table, his feet braced on the overturned bench, looking out the tilting galley window into the darkening sky rolling itself down to hills of gray water which flung foam and strands of feathery seaweed against the glass.

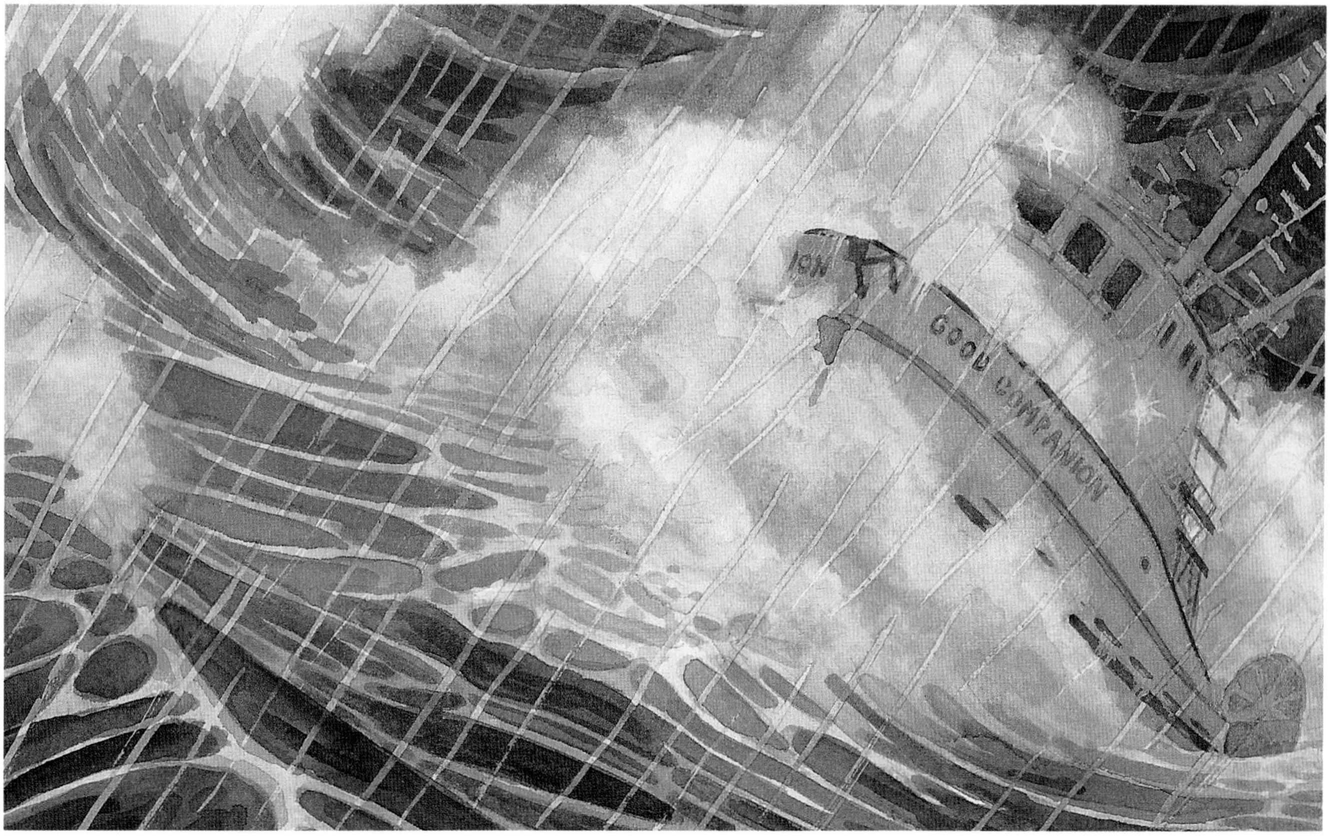
GOOD COMPANION

The *Good Companion* fell heavily into the trough between the waves and began to take on water. Her decks were awash, hatches filling, stern sinking. The captain leaned into the wheel and hung on as a mountain of water climbed beside the starboard bow.

In the rush of water and wind-driven spray falling toward him, the captain was certain he saw the redheaded girl. Her hands were outstretched. Her hair swirled around her like seaweed in the foaming sea.

"Hold on!" the captain roared, and the deckhands strained to keep the steering wheel steady as he burst open the wheelhouse door.

On the slanting deck, the captain leaned over the side to reach again and again into the salt cold swells, trying to grasp the girl he could no longer see. The *Good Companion* heeled hard under his feet and lay on her side, hesitating.

Safe harbors, dock ladders, bakeries, fish prices, front porches and all other memories of land spun away from the captain and his crew. They were on their knees, clinging to ladders and railings, watching water rise around them.

"Come back. Oh, come back," the captain whispered, not knowing if he was calling the land or the redheaded girl he was no longer sure he had seen or the *Good Companion* herself.

The world of waves and wind, of night sky and distant land, stopped for the men on the *Good Companion*. They could no longer hear the sound of the storm. To them, the heaving sea seemed almost still. They waited to go down.

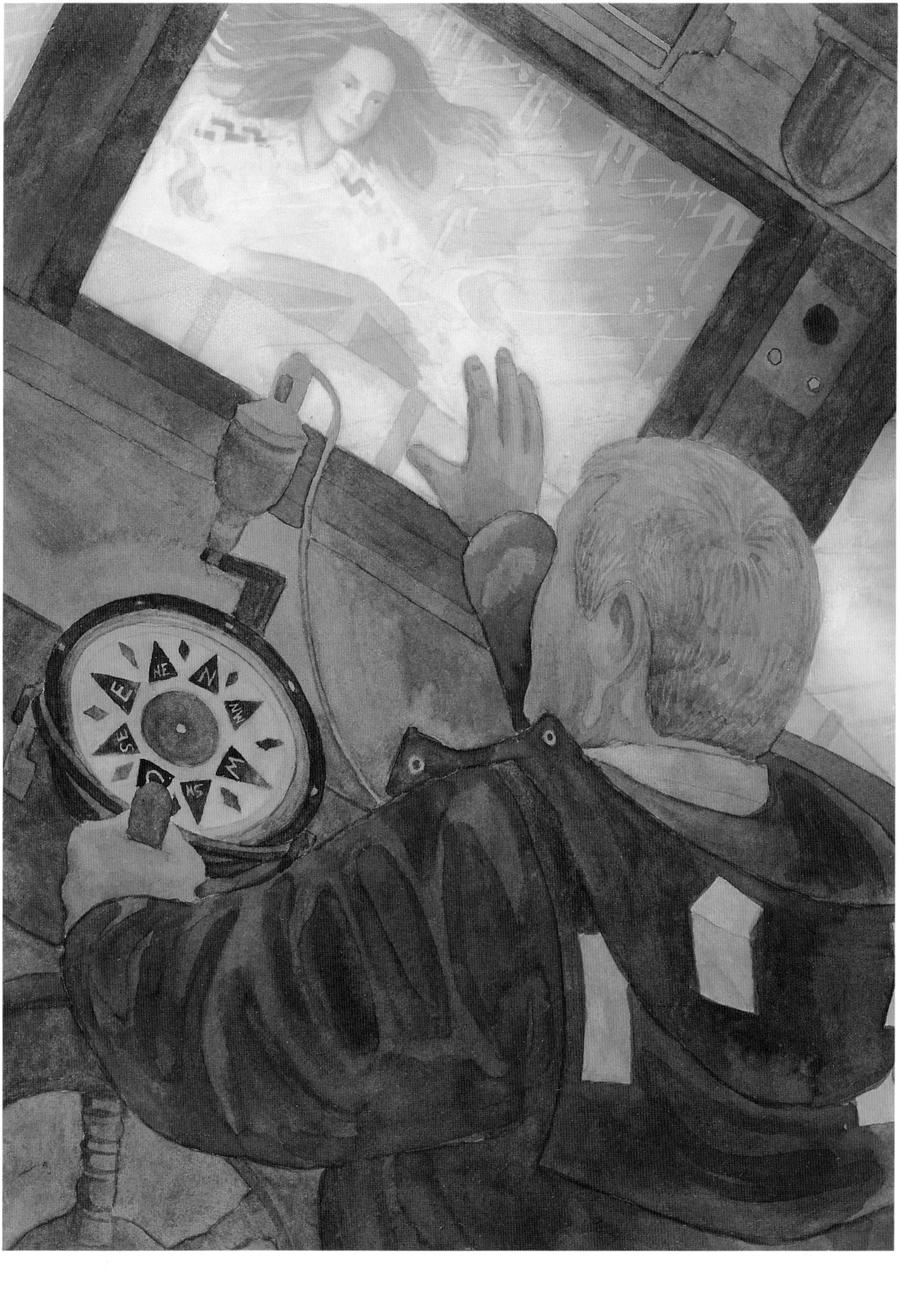

The captain heard the beating of great wings behind him on the flooding starboard deck. He saw only the deep water almost touching the deckrail, then he felt the *Good Companion* rolling slowly upright, bow into the wind. The sea still surged high, but when the captain took the wheel again, his boat rode the heavy swells like a bird.

Down below the engineer blessed his pumps, as seawater poured from the decks and hatches.

The deckhands picked up broken dishes in the galley. "Only one lucky cup left," the youngest deckhand said. "It must have held just enough luck to save us." He hung the surviving cup on a hook over the sink, facing inboard.

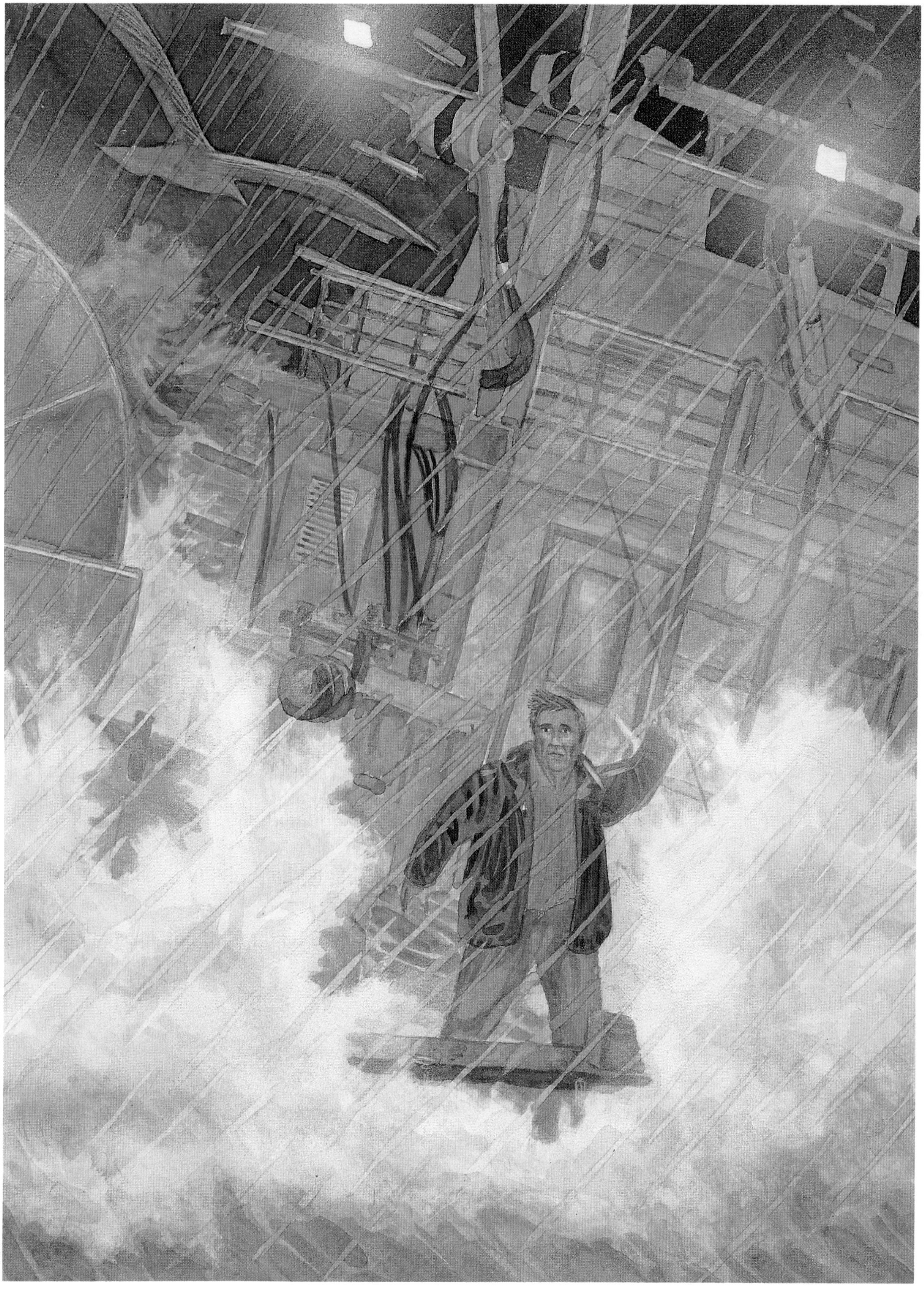

The cook found the coffee pot where it had rolled behind the stove, and fitted on its lid. He stepped into the wheelhouse, darkened for steering at night, and stood beside the captain. "Was it luck?" he asked.

The captain looked at him. "More than luck," he said.

Both men peered into the blackness that had joined sea and sky together around the *Good Companion* as she rose and fell, jogging steadily in the still-wild waves. They said no more about luck or the strangeness of saviors beyond luck.

The captain spoke quietly. "When the tide slacks, we'll turn back to the bay before morning."

"I might as well wait to fix dinner when we quit rolling then. The ham went overboard anyway."

"You could make spaghetti for a change," the captain said.

"Change?" the cook asked. "You want a change?"

"We could use some changes here," the captain told him. "Maybe we'll try new grounds tomorrow when this gale blows out."

The cook smiled and closed the wheelhouse door after himself. He filled the coffee pot at the sink, watching the yellow light from the galley flowing over the hills of dark water moving outside the *Good Companion*'s windows.

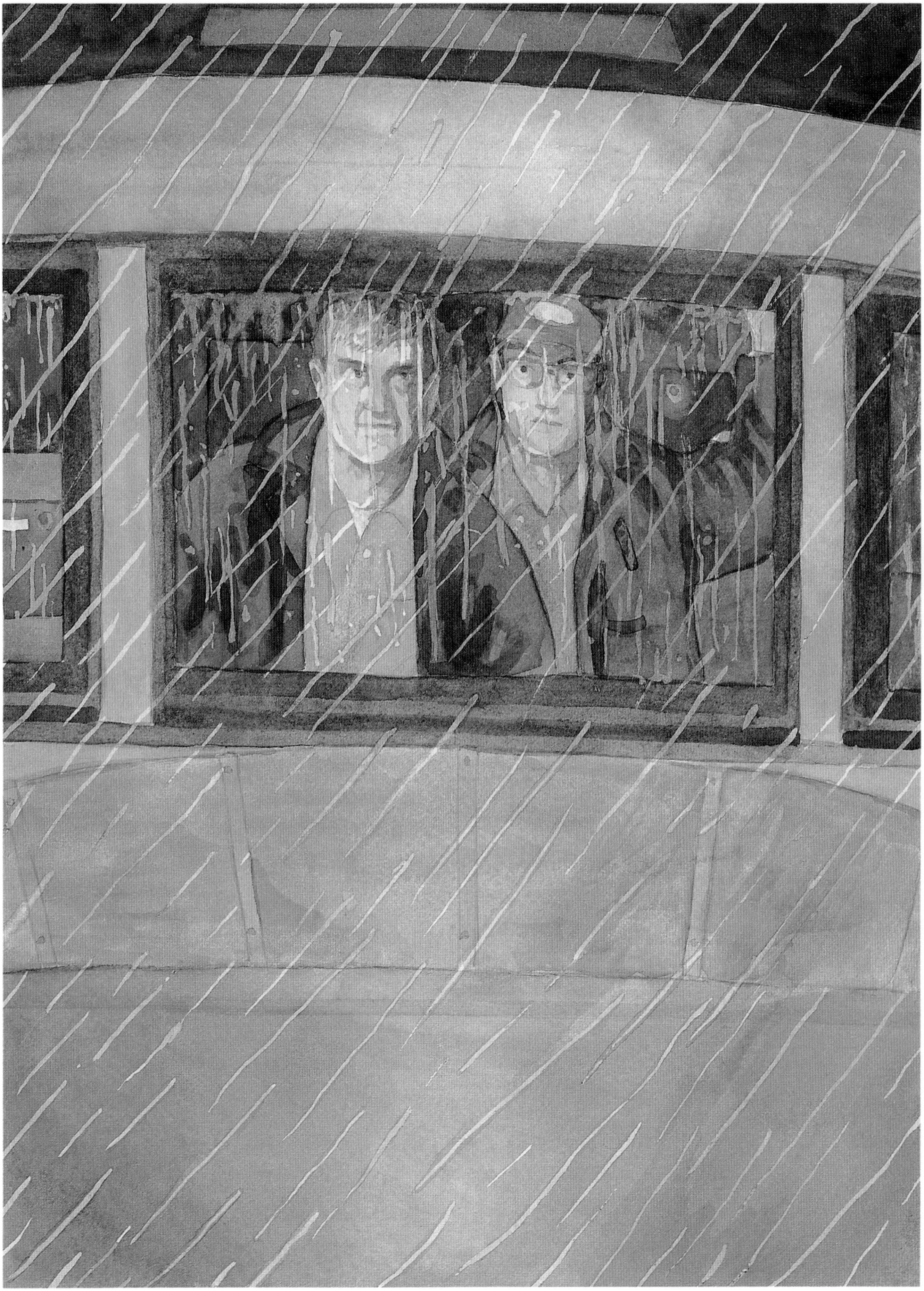

For British Columbia deep-sea trawlers.
J.S.

For my good companions, June and Lara.
S.M.

Text copyright © 1998 Joan Skogan
Illustration copyright © 1998 Stephen McCallum

Canadian Cataloguing in Publication Data
Skogan, Joan, 1945–
The good companion

ISBN 1-55143-134-3

I. McCallum, Stephen, 1960– II. Title.
PS8587.K58G66 1998 jC813'.54 C97-911112-9
PZ7.S628352Go 1998

Library of Congress Catalog Card Number: 97-81072

Orca Book Publishers gratefully acknowledges the support
of our publishing programs provided by the following
agencies: the Department of Canadian Heritage, The
Canada Council for the Arts, and the British Columbia
Ministry of Small Business, Tourism and Culture.

Cover design by Christine Toller

Printed and bound in Canada

Orca Book Publishers
PO Box 5626, Station B
Victoria, BC Canada
V8R 6S4

Orca Book Publishers
PO Box 468
Custer, WA USA
98240-0468

98 99 00 5 4 3 2 1